Penguin  Readers

FOOL ME ONCE

HARLAN COBEN

LEVEL
5

RETOLD BY PRAKASH PARMAR
ILLUSTRATED BY BETSY FALCO
SERIES EDITOR: SORREL PITTS

Contains adult content, which could include: sexual behaviour or exploitation, misuse of alcohol, smoking, illegal drugs, violence and dangerous behaviour.

This book includes content that may be distressing to readers, including descriptions of suicide or self-harm.

PENGUIN BOOKS

UK | USA | Canada | Ireland | Australia
India | New Zealand | South Africa

Penguin Books is part of the Penguin Random House group of companies whose addresses can be found at global.penguinrandomhouse.com.
www.penguin.co.uk www.puffin.co.uk www.ladybird.co.uk

Fool Me Once first published by Penguin Books Ltd, 2016
This Penguin Readers edition published by Penguin Books Ltd, 2026
001

Original text written by Harlan Coben
Text for Penguin Readers edition adapted by Prakash Parmar
Original copyright © Harlan Coben, 2016
Text for Penguin Readers edition copyright © Penguin Books Ltd, 2026
Illustrated by Betsy Falco
Illustrations copyright © Penguin Books Ltd, 2026
Cover image copyright © Penguin Books Ltd, 2026

The moral right of the original author has been asserted

Penguin Random House values and supports copyright. Copyright fuels creativity, encourages diverse voices, promotes freedom of expression and supports a vibrant culture. Thank you for purchasing an authorized edition of this book and for respecting intellectual property laws by not reproducing, scanning or distributing any part of it by any means without permission. You are supporting authors and enabling Penguin Random House to continue to publish books for everyone. No part of this book may be used or reproduced in any manner for the purpose of training artificial intelligence technologies or systems. In accordance with Article 4(3) of the DSM Directive 2019/790, Penguin Random House expressly reserves this work from the text and data mining exception.

Printed and bound in Great Britain by Clays Ltd, Elcograf S.p.A.

The authorized representative in the EEA is Penguin Random House Ireland,
Morrison Chambers, 32 Nassau Street, Dublin D02 YH68

A CIP catalogue record for this book is available from the British Library

ISBN: 978–0–241–75399–6

All correspondence to:
Penguin Books
Penguin Random House Children's
One Embassy Gardens, 8 Viaduct Gardens,
London SW11 7BW

Penguin Random House is committed to a sustainable future for our business, our readers and our planet. This book is made from Forest Stewardship Council® certified

Contents

Note about the story	4
Before-reading questions	4
Chapter One – Joe's funeral	5
Chapter Two – Maya checks the nanny cam	12
Chapter Three – An attack	19
Chapter Four – A visit to Eileen	27
Chapter Five – Family secrets	31
Chapter Six – Corey the whistleblower	39
Chapter Seven – Looking for Tom Douglass	46
Chapter Eight – Two more deaths	51
Chapter Nine – Visiting Philadelphia	57
Chapter Ten – Finding Tom Douglass	63
Chapter Eleven – What happened to Andrew?	67
Chapter Twelve – Finding Isabella	72
Chapter Thirteen – The truth about the Burketts	77
Chapter Fourteen – Twenty-five years later	84
During-reading questions	86
After-reading questions	88
Exercises	89
Project work	93
Glossary	93

Note about the story

Fool Me Once is about Maya, whose husband, Joe, was murdered in Central Park in New York City. Joe belonged to the very rich Burkett family. One day, Maya sees something on her **nanny cam*** that makes her question everything that she believes.

Maya is an **ex-soldier** who used to fly **military combat helicopters**. Like many other soldiers, she has **PTSD** from her experiences in the army. Her military **career** ended when a **whistleblower** put a video online. The video was recorded by Maya's helicopter camera in Iraq.

Maya lives in New Jersey, which is not far from New York City. She visits different towns in the **state**, like Livingston and Paterson, and also goes to Philadelphia, the largest city in the state of Pennsylvania.

Fool Me Once is now a series on Netflix, where the story happens in Britain instead of the United States of America.

Before-reading questions

1 Look at the "Note about the story". What do you know about whistleblowers? Why do they put videos online?

2 Look at the definition of "nanny cam" on page 95. Why do people have these, do you think?

3 What do you know about the war in Iraq? Why do soldiers like Maya get PTSD from their experiences in wars?

*Definitions of words in **bold** can be found in the glossary on pages 93–96.

CHAPTER ONE
Joe's funeral

Joe's **funeral** was three days after his murder.

Maya was wearing an uncomfortable black dress. She had been to over a hundred funerals, but this was the first time that she had had to wear black, and she hated it. Joe would not like it, either. He preferred her **military** clothes, when she had been Army **Captain** Maya Stern.

He had been so handsome. They had gotten married just one year after meeting, and Lily came not long after that.

To her right, Joe's family — his mother, Judith, his brother, Neil, and his sister, Caroline — looked tired and sad. To her left, her (and Joe's) two-year-old daughter, Lily, was getting bored.

There were hundreds of people at the funeral, and Maya thought, "Joe would like this." Joe liked people. People liked Joe. But many of them were also here because the story had received a lot of attention. Joe belonged to the great Burkett family, and he was the husband of a woman who had been **involved** in a well-known **scandal**.

Judith Burkett took Maya's hand. "This," she said, "is even worse than Andrew's funeral."

It was the second time that Judith had been at the funeral of one of her children. Two of her three sons were now dead. The first one, Andrew, had died in an accident. Maya looked down at Lily, and thought about Judith's pain.

"It's my **fault**," Maya said. She had not planned to say it. Judith looked at her.

"There was nothing that you could do," Judith replied, although there was something strange in her voice. Maya understood what it was, because others were probably thinking the same thing. They were thinking that Army Captain Maya Stern had saved many people in the past, so why couldn't she save her own husband?

Maya thought about the night in Central Park, with the gun, the sound of **shots**, and Joe falling. There had been blood all over her shirt as she ran out of the park, calling for help.

She closed her eyes and told herself, "Don't think about it now."

At the end of the funeral, all the guests came to say goodbye to her. The last people to come were her sister's husband, Eddie, and Daniel and Alexa, her nephew and niece. But Maya's sister, Claire, was not here, because four months ago someone had murdered her, too.

Maya said to Alexa, "Sorry that I missed your last soccer match, but I'll be there tomorrow."

"Oh, you don't have to come," Eddie said.

"It's OK. It'll be nice to have something to do," said Maya.

Maya **hugged** Eddie, Alexa, and Daniel and was watching them go back to their car when she noticed the New York Police detective Roger Kierce standing by a tree. He was **investigating** Joe's murder. She thought about going to talk to him, but decided not to.

Then, Eileen, Maya's oldest friend, drove her and Lily home. Lily fell asleep in the car, so, when they got to the house, Maya carefully carried her out of the car.

"Can I come in?" Eileen asked. "I want to give you something."

Inside the house, Maya held the gift in her hand. "A **digital picture frame**?" she asked.

"Yes, and I've already put some photos of your family on it. But it's also a **nanny cam**. There's a secret camera inside," Eileen said. "When you're at work, you want to be sure that Lily is safe, don't you?"

"Well, yes," Maya said.

Eileen took the picture frame back from Maya and put it on the bookshelf in Lily's playroom. "The camera will take a video of the whole room, but it only records when people are moving," she explained. "Lily's **nanny** was at the funeral, wasn't she?"

"Isabella?" Maya asked. "Yes, she was with her mother and brother. Her mother used to be Joe's nanny and her brother, Hector, is the Burketts' gardener."

"Do you trust her?" Eileen asked.

"I suppose so. You know me," Maya said.

"Yes, I do know you," Eileen replied. "You trust no one, Maya. And we're thinking about your child. That's why I'm giving you this. When you want to watch the video, you take the **SD card** out of the picture frame and put it in your computer."

Maya smiled. "I don't know why I didn't think of this myself," she said.

"Call me if you need anything," Eileen said, moving to the door and opening it. "Oh, someone is here to see you." She hugged Maya and left.

The visitor was Detective Roger Kierce.

"I know that it's not a great day to visit," he said, "but you're going back to work tomorrow, aren't you? I just want to discuss the night of the murder again."

Maya was unsure what to think about Kierce, which was probably what he wanted. "Come in then. What would you like to know?" she asked.

"Let's start at the beginning," said Kierce, taking a notebook out of his pocket. "Why did you meet Joe in Central Park that night?"

"We were talking on the phone, and he said that he wanted to meet there," Maya replied.

"Was this normal?" asked Kierce.

"We used to go there sometimes, yes," Maya replied. "It's a nice place."

"You described two men wearing black **ski masks** who came into the park. Am I correct?"

"Yes."

"You said that one man wore a black sweater, jeans, and red shoes. He was the one who shot your husband. The other man wore a light blue T-shirt and black running shoes, and they both had guns," said Kierce.

"That's correct," she replied.

"You said that they wanted to rob you, but Joe was slow to give them his money and his watch. Why was that?"

"Have you ever had a gun pointing at your face, Detective?" asked Maya.

"No."

"Then maybe you don't understand," she said. "When someone points a gun at you, sometimes you can't move because of the shock, which is what happened to Joe."

They were both silent for several moments.

"Perhaps it was an accident, and the robber didn't really plan to shoot?" asked Kierce.

"No, it wasn't," replied Maya. "It's not an accident when you shoot someone three times."

Kierce nodded and checked his notes. "The first **bullet** was in your husband's left shoulder and the second hit him near his neck, although those shots didn't kill him. So what happened next?"

"I already told you," she said. "I tried to hold Joe. He fell on to his knees ... I didn't see the third shot."

"That's right," Kierce said, slowly. "Because you were running away."

Inside her head, Maya suddenly heard the sound of guns, a **helicopter**, and people screaming. She shut her eyes and took a few deep breaths. "Yes, I ran. OK? I ran away from two men with guns and left my husband."

She stopped.

"No one is **blaming** you, Maya."

"I know that, Detective," said Maya, angrily.

Kierce looked at his notes. "You said that the gun that killed Joe was a Smith and Wesson 686 **revolver** and the other guy had a Beretta M9. You remember these details very well."

"I was in the army," said Maya. "I know about guns."

"You also own several, and isn't one of them a Smith and Wesson 686?" he asked.

"Yes, but you know that already. According to New Jersey **state** law, I have to report all the guns that I buy, so of course you checked that immediately after Joe's death. So can we stop playing games and hurry up?" she said.

"From where Joe fell, how long does it take to leave the park?" Kierce asked.

The change of question surprised Maya. "I'm sure that you already know," she said.

"Yes, I do," he said. "I can run out of the park in one minute. But you're younger and healthier than me, and it took you longer. We talked to some people outside the park who said that they saw you running out at least a minute or two after the third shot. How do you explain that?"

"Do you think that I shot my husband, Detective?"

"Did you shoot him?" he asked.

"No," she said. "And I can **prove** it. I train with guns all the time, and I wouldn't need three shots to kill a man."

Kierce actually smiled. "Can you show me your guns?" he asked.

They went down to the **basement**, where Maya showed Kierce her gun **safe**. "You have to use your **fingerprint** on the lock," said Maya. "Only Joe and I could open it."

Maya opened the safe, which had several different guns inside. "Here's the Smith and Wesson 686 revolver."

"May I take it with me?" he asked.

"Why?" she asked.

"Don't worry. I don't think that you shot your husband," he said.

"Detective," said Maya, "you're not telling me something."

Kierce smiled. "I'll contact you soon."

CHAPTER TWO
Maya checks the nanny cam

Isabella, Lily's nanny, arrived at seven o'clock the next morning. Lily jumped out of her chair and ran toward Isabella, who picked her up and hugged her.

Maya kissed Lily goodbye and drove to work. Sometimes, she felt guilty for not spending enough time with her daughter. She loved Lily, but she had never wanted just to stay at home and be a mother. And, after her experiences in the army, it was harder to live in this ordinary world. When she spent time with other mothers, while they discussed their children, her mind went back to the soldiers that she saw dying. How could this world of babies and **day care** be the same as that other world of war and killing?

Maya knew that she had some kind of **PTSD** from being in the war in Iraq, although the truth was that all soldiers came back with problems.

Maya had flown military **combat helicopters**, which shot **missiles** to help the soldiers on the ground. She had planned to fly combat helicopters her whole life, but, when Corey Rudzinski's website **released** that video to the world, the scandal ended her **career** as a soldier. So now she taught people to fly planes.

After work, Maya went to watch Alexa's soccer game. She was driving her niece home after the match when she noticed a red car behind her. It followed her for a while, but when she arrived at Claire's house it carried on down the road. It looked like any ordinary car.

A week later, Maya was driving home from work when she saw the red car behind her again. "This is definitely not happening by chance," she thought. What should she do? While she was thinking about her possible options, the car disappeared down another road.

When Maya got home, Hector was waiting outside by his truck, wearing a sweater although it was a hot day. He usually picked Isabella up after he finished work.

Inside, Lily was sitting beside Isabella on the couch, drawing. Isabella stood up.

"How was she today?" Maya asked her.

"She was lovely," said Isabella, looking at Lily sadly. "She knows nothing about her father's death."

"I'll see you in the morning," said Maya.

"Yes, Mrs. Burkett."

Maya sat on the couch next to her daughter and looked at the nanny cam, remembering that they were being recorded. She checked it most days, but she never saw anything to worry her. Isabella was always smiling and playing with Lily.

Maya's phone rang. It was Shane, her best friend from the army. They had flown helicopters in Iraq together, and now he was in the military police.

"How are you feeling?" he asked.

"Fine," she said.

"We need to talk," he said. "Can I come to your house? I'll bring some pizza."

When Shane arrived, the three of them ate the pizza together. After Lily was in bed, Maya and Shane got some cold beers from the fridge.

"So what do you want to talk about?" asked Maya.

"I've heard that Corey Rudzinski may be back," Shane said.

He waited for Maya to react, but she drank her beer and said nothing.

Corey Rudzinski was a **whistleblower** who owned a website called CoreyTheWhistle.com. The website released videos of information that some people wanted to **hide**. If the **government**, the police, or a company did something wrong, Corey's website would tell the world about it.

And what would happen if a soldier flying a military combat helicopter killed a group of **civilians** by accident?

Yes, Corey had released that information about Maya, but since then he had disappeared.

"Maya?" Shane said.

"He can't hurt me any more," she said. "He's already released the video from our helicopter camera."

"Except," said Shane, "he didn't release the **audio**. Why was that, do you think?"

"I suppose that you have an idea?" she said.

Shane nodded. "I think that he's keeping it for the right time. He released the video and got everyone's attention.

Then, when they start forgetting about it, he'll release the audio. He needs the attention for his website to be a success."

"Shane," said Maya. "I don't care. I'm not in the army any more and my husband is dead. Corey can do what he likes." Except she did care more than Shane realized. He did not know the whole truth about the video.

Shane drank his beer. "So are you going to tell me what's really going on?" he asked. "A couple of weeks ago, I did that test on the bullet for you without asking questions. Why did you need me to do that? Did you know that Joe was in

danger? Or was it really *you* that they were trying to kill?"

Maya closed her eyes. She could hear the sound of helicopters and screaming.

"Maya?" Shane's voice was quiet. "Are you going to try to find Joe's killers yourself?" he asked.

Maya gave no reply.

"I'm here if you need me," he said. "You know that, don't you?"

"Yes," she said. "Do you trust me, Shane?"

"I trust you with my life," he said.

"Then don't ask me any more questions."

Shane finished his beer and got up. Maya followed him to the door.

"I need one more favor," she said, handing him a piece of paper with a car **license plate** written on it. "Can you find the owner of this red car for me?"

Shane looked unhappy, but he took the paper, kissed her on the head and left.

Maya went upstairs to check Lily and then went to the home gym to exercise, which helped her relax.

Later, she sat in front of her computer and went to Corey Rudzinski's whistleblower website, CoreyTheWhistle.com. It was full of videos with titles like "The top ten ways that the government is watching you" and "Do you really think that the police are there to help you?" She searched for the video from the combat helicopter that she and Shane had flown during the war in Iraq and pressed "Play."

Four soldiers on the ground had already died, and Maya

and Shane were trying to save the last two, who were still alive but being attacked by the enemy. A black car was driving toward them to kill them, and Maya and Shane could hear the two young soldiers on their radios crying for help. But, before shooting a missile at the black car, Maya had to wait for a radio message from the guys back at the army camp. They needed to check that there were no civilians in the car. Because of all the noise, it was difficult to hear the message from the camp, so it was unclear whether they ought to wait or not. When she heard the two soldiers scream, Maya decided to shoot a missile at the car, **destroying** it. The soldiers were saved. It seemed like the right thing to do at the time.

There was no audio to go with the video that Maya was now watching, but later, in bed, the sounds came back. She switched off the light and waited. First, she felt hot. Then, there were the pictures in her mind. But the worst thing was the awful noise of helicopters, guns, and, of course, the soldiers screaming.

She found her sleeping pills and took two of them. They did not stop the sounds, but they made them a little quieter, so that finally she could sleep.

Maya woke at five o'clock the next morning, as she always did. She went downstairs, noticed the nanny cam, and decided to watch yesterday's video. So she took the SD card out of the digital picture frame and put it in her computer.

The video showed Lily and Isabella together on the couch. Then, Maya noticed something strange.

The video suddenly went dark because someone was standing in front of the camera. Was it Isabella? But Isabella was wearing a red blouse yesterday, while this shirt was green.

The person on the camera moved, and Maya could just see Lily sitting on the couch. Then, the person appeared again.

It was a man.

In the video, Lily looked up at the man and smiled. Maya went cold. Lily only smiled when she knew someone. Maybe it was Hector, Isabella's brother? But he was wearing a gray sweatshirt yesterday, Maya remembered.

Then, the man sat down on the couch, and Maya saw his face. She did not scream, but it was hard to breathe.

There, on the computer, Maya watched Lily sitting next to her dead husband.

CHAPTER THREE
An attack

The video did not last long. "Joe" stood up and carried Lily away from the camera. Then, the video stopped. The next time that the camera started recording, Isabella and Lily were playing, and the rest of the video was the same.

Maya watched the video again twice, and then she went upstairs to Joe's closet and stopped at the door. She had not opened it since his death. Joe almost always hated the clothes that Maya bought for him, except for one green shirt that she had given him as a gift. She knew where it was.

But the green shirt was gone. Someone had taken it.

Ten minutes later, Maya looked out of the bedroom window and watched closely as Isabella walked through the front door. Did she look more worried today, or was Maya imagining it? She went downstairs and into the kitchen, where Isabella was washing up a cup.

"Isabella?" said Maya. "May I talk to you?"

Isabella looked up in surprise. "Now, Mrs. Burkett?"

"Yes, please," Maya said. Her own voice suddenly sounded strange to her. "I'd like to show you something."

Isabella moved slowly toward Maya, looking a little scared.

"Did anyone come here yesterday?" asked Maya.

"No, Mrs. Burkett."

"I want to show you something on the computer," interrupted Maya. "I keep a camera in the playroom, which records everything that happens when I'm not here. A friend gave it to me."

Isabella looked confused.

"But I never saw a camera, Mrs. Burkett," she said.

"It's a secret camera," said Maya. "It's inside that new digital picture frame."

"So you're secretly watching me. You don't trust me," Isabella said.

"It's not about you, Isabella. I want my child to be safe. But watch this."

Maya played the video on the computer without watching it again. Instead, she watched Isabella's face and tried to stay calm. The **fake** Joe appeared in the video.

"Well? Did you see that man in the video?" asked Maya.

Isabella said nothing.

"You saw him, didn't you?" said Maya.

"Who?"

"Joe!" Maya held Isabella's shirt. "How did Joe get into my house?"

"Please, Mrs. Burkett! You're scaring me!" said Isabella. "Are you telling me that you saw Joe in that video?"

"Mommy …"

Lily was standing at the door to the kitchen. Maya looked toward her daughter, and Isabella took this chance to move away.

"It's OK, Lily," Maya said. She looked back at Isabella.

AN ATTACK

"I want answers," she said.

Isabella nodded. "OK, but I need some water first."

Maya turned away to get her some water. When she turned back, she screamed as a terrible pain filled her eyes, and she fell to her knees. Isabella had used **pepper spray** on her, burning her eyes, nose, and mouth and making it difficult to breathe. Maya could not move, but she heard the sound of someone running and the door closing. Isabella was gone.

Ten minutes later, the pain finally started to disappear and Maya managed to get up to wash her eyes.

"Mommy?"

"Mommy's fine, Lily," she said. "Draw a picture for me. I'll be there in a minute."

Maya was extremely angry, mostly with herself. Stupidly, she had turned her back on her enemy. She had to find Isabella. But just then the doorbell rang.

Detective Kierce stared at her when she opened the door. "What happened to you?" he said.

"It's pepper spray," she said. "My nanny, Isabella, used it on me."

"Why?" he asked.

"I saw something on my nanny cam," she said.

Kierce looked confused, so she took him to her computer. But, when she pressed the play button, there was nothing there. Then, she discovered that the SD card was gone. It was not on the floor, either.

"What?" asked Kierce.

Maya took slow, deep breaths. She needed to stay calm and think carefully. "Isabella has taken the SD card," she said.

"What was on it?" he asked.

"You won't believe me," she said. "I saw Joe."

Kierce was quiet for several moments.

"So it was an old video?" he said. "It was recorded when Joe was alive?"

"I didn't get the camera until after Joe's murder, and the

AN ATTACK

video has yesterday's date on it," she said.

"You know that's impossible," he said.

"I do," she said.

They stared at each other.

"So why are you here?" Maya asked.

"I need you to come to the police station."

There was a **day care center** not far from her house, where Maya took Lily before going with Kierce to the station. He took her into a room with a glass window that showed another room.

"I want you to look at some people for me," he said. Then, he called to someone outside the room. "Bring in the first group!"

Six people walked into the other room wearing ski masks. They could not see Maya or Kierce because for them the window was a mirror.

"Mrs. Burkett," Kierce said, "do you know any of these men?"

Maya looked carefully at their clothes and size and pointed to the one who looked like Joe's killer. Then, six more men came in, and Maya was sure that the other guy from Central Park was in this second group.

"Yesterday, we brought in two men who might be Joe's killers," Kierce explained. "Look at this." He played her a video from a store **security camera** near Central Park on the night of Joe's murder, which showed two men buying some drinks. One of them clearly had a gun in his jacket.

"We searched their homes and found the clothes that you described," Kierce said. "We also found one gun, a Beretta M9, but we didn't find the Smith and Wesson 686 revolver that killed your husband."

"Maybe they threw it away?" said Maya.

"That could be true. Except guys like these don't throw away expensive guns, because they prefer to sell them for the cash."

"But there was a lot of media interest in Joe's murder," she said. "So maybe they thought that it was too dangerous to keep it?"

"That's possible," he said.

"But you have another idea, don't you?" she asked.

"Yes," said Kierce, "although it's a crazy one. We checked the bullets from your husband's body. They're from the same gun as another murder."

"So these guys have killed before," said Maya.

"The same gun doesn't mean the same killers. And one of the guys was in prison at the time of the first murder," said Kierce.

"When was the first murder?" asked Maya.

"Four months ago."

The room went cold. Maya knew what Kierce would say next. He nodded and said, "The same gun that killed your husband also killed your sister."

They were both silent. "Are you OK?" Kierce asked.

"I'm fine," said Maya.

AN ATTACK

"OK, we need to look at this in a whole new way," he said, opening his notebook. "The two murders seemed to be completely separate, but now we know that the same gun was used for both of them. We know that you were in Iraq when your sister was killed, and we've checked your Smith and Wesson 686 revolver. It wasn't the gun that was used in Joe's murder, so his killer couldn't be you."

"So before you checked that, you thought that I could be the killer?" asked Maya.

"You have to understand, Maya," said Kierce. "When someone is murdered, we always have to investigate the husband or wife."

"OK, so you've done that. Now what do we do?" she asked.

"We look for **connections**," Kierce said, "between your sister and your husband."

"The biggest connection is me," said Maya, "although they also worked together."

"Yes," said Kierce. "Joe gave Claire a job in the family company. Did they have any problems working together?"

"No," she said. "They liked it. They talked on the phone about the company all the time, although actually I wasn't in the country most of the time, so I don't really know."

At that moment another police officer came in and spoke quietly to Kierce. Maya watched. Why had Kierce not talked to her about the nanny cam video? After the conversation he came toward her.

"What's wrong?" she asked.

He picked up his coat. "I'll drive you home, and we can talk in the car."

Ten minutes later, in the car, Kierce said, "That conversation with the other officer was about you and the secret camera and pepper spray."

So he had not forgotten about it.

"You said that your nanny attacked you with pepper spray, and we saw that your eyes were red," he said. "So we sent a police officer to her house."

"And did you find her?" she asked.

Kierce kept looking at the road. "Let me ask you a question first. During that conversation, did you attack her?"

"Is that what she told the police?" asked Maya. "No, I didn't. Did she talk about the video?"

"Yes," Kierce said. "She said that you'd seen Joe on the video, but when you played it to her, there was nothing there."

"Wow," Maya said.

"She said that you're becoming **paranoid** and starting to imagine things. She also said that you attacked her first, and that you always carry a gun, so she was scared. That's why she used the pepper spray."

"And what about the SD card?" asked Maya.

"She said that she knows nothing about it."

But Isabella had taken it. So she had lied. Isabella was part of it.

But part of what?

CHAPTER FOUR
A visit to Eileen

At home, Maya thought of something else. Why had Eileen given her the nanny cam? It helped to make you feel safe, but could someone use it to secretly watch you as well? Or was she just being paranoid? Maya heard Eileen's voice.

"You trust no one, Maya."

But she trusted Shane, and she had trusted Claire. Did she also trust Eileen? Maya needed to **find out**.

Eileen was in her front garden working on her roses when Maya arrived.

"Hey, you!" she said, looking up.

"Why did you give me that secret camera?" asked Maya.

Eileen stopped what she was doing. "Because your husband was murdered, and you have a young daughter. Why? What happened?"

"Where did you buy it?" asked Maya.

"Online," said Eileen.

"Show me," said Maya.

Eileen angrily pulled off her gardening gloves. "Fine," she said, and they went inside the house.

Eileen, Claire, and Maya had been friends in college. Maya had liked Eileen because she was wild and fun. But that was before she met Robby, who was now her **ex-husband**. He had been kind to her at first, but then started changing. Maya had noticed marks on Eileen's body, and realized that Robby was hurting her. Then, one night, Eileen sent Maya a text message that said: *He's going to kill me.* Maya immediately took her gun and went to Eileen's house. Robby moved out after that.

"You scared Robby a lot that night," said Eileen, "and you saved my life. But, after you went back to Iraq, he started coming here again, and I was scared. I thought about getting a gun, but I didn't want to be sent to prison for killing him, so I bought the camera to secretly record him attacking me. He stopped coming after he knew that I had that video."

Eileen showed Maya the email from the online store where she had bought three nanny cams a month ago. She had given one of them to Maya. Maya had no reason not to believe her.

"Maya," said Eileen. "I'm cross that you didn't trust me, but let's forget about that now. What's going on?"

"I saw something ..." Maya began. Then, she changed her mind. It would take too long to explain about seeing Joe, and Eileen could not help her with it anyway.

"The police have learned that the same gun killed Claire and Joe," she said instead. Eileen's eyes opened wide with shock.

"So I need you to think back," continued Maya. "You knew Claire better than anyone. Maybe she and Joe were involved in something dangerous. Was there anything strange going on?"

Eileen looked down. "I didn't think that it mattered at

the time, but Claire and I were having dinner one evening when she got a phone call. We never had secrets from each other, except this time Claire looked nervous and went outside to answer the call. When she came back, she said it was nothing, but she wouldn't tell me who she talked to."

"Well, the police probably checked her phone after she died," said Maya.

"Except that's the problem," said Eileen. "Claire's phone was still on the table when she went outside. She was talking on a second phone."

Before trying to find Claire's second phone, Maya visited Isabella's home to try to speak to her. She lived with her mother and brother in a small house near the Burketts' home.

Maya parked outside and knocked on the door, but no one answered. Then, a truck drove up behind her and parked. Hector got out and stared at her.

"Where's Isabella?" Maya asked him. "I just want to talk to her and say sorry."

The front door then opened. It was Rosa, Isabella's mother. "She's not here," said Rosa, "so leave. Come inside, Hector."

Hector went inside, and Rosa shut the door in Maya's face.

As Maya went back to her car, Shane called her. He had checked the license plate of the red car and found the company which had rented it to someone, although he could not get the driver's name.

After **hanging up**, Maya went to Claire's house. Nobody was home, so she unlocked the door with her key and went inside. Claire had died four months ago, and the hall was still full of boxes of her stuff, which Eddie had not moved.

So what had happened to that phone?

Maya searched through the boxes, which was a painful experience because everything **reminded** her of Claire's life. But there was no phone in any of them. Then, Maya remembered something. When they were in high school, Claire had started smoking, and their dad had hated it. So she used to hide her cigarettes in a piece of furniture that had belonged to their grandmother, and which was now in Claire's living room. There was a secret **compartment** at the bottom of it where their grandmother used to hide her gold and cash. When Maya clicked the lock and opened this secret compartment, the phone was inside. She smiled to herself.

Back at home, Maya switched on the phone and checked the past phone calls. There were sixteen calls, all to the same number. Was Claire having secret meetings with someone? She searched the phone number online.

It was for a business in the north part of New Jersey state, a **strip club** called Leather and Lace. This was even more confusing. Was Claire secretly working there? There was only one way to find out the truth. Maya would go to Leather and Lace tomorrow.

CHAPTER FIVE
Family secrets

The next morning, Maya woke up to the same noise in her head of helicopters, guns, and screams. She closed her eyes and waited for them to disappear. Then, she got out of bed and got ready to go to the Burketts' home. Today was the meeting with the family lawyer to read Joe's **will**.

She took Lily to the day care center and drove to the Burketts' house. When she switched on the radio, they were talking about Corey Rudzinski on the news.

"Corey Rudzinski has promised that he has plenty of new information to release to the world that will definitely end some people's careers," Maya heard.

Despite telling Shane that she did not care, this news frightened her. Corey still had the audio from her video to release.

The Burketts' home was huge, like the kind of rich person's house that you see in movies. Maya drove through the gate and up a hill past the family's private soccer field. Joe's mother, Judith, was waiting outside the house for her. She was a beautiful, clever, and rich woman, who still got attention from men. Maya got out of the car, and she and Judith kissed each other on the cheek. "You need to make things better with Isabella," said Judith.

"You can help me with that if you tell me where she is," said Maya.

"I don't know, but I understand that she's traveling. Let me be direct, Maya," said Judith. "Your husband was murdered and you saw it happen. You're now taking care of your daughter alone and you still have PTSD. It's clear to me that you need to see a doctor and get some help."

"I'm fine, Judith," said Maya.

A voice said, "Mom?"

Judith turned around. It was Caroline, Joe's sister. While Judith was a strong woman, her daughter was the opposite and always looked a little scared.

After kissing Caroline, Maya followed her and Judith into the library, where Neil, Joe's youngest brother, was waiting. Joe had been the oldest, and the middle brother, Andrew, had died at sea. Neil was the youngest son, and, although Joe was the first child, their father had made Neil the boss of the Burkett family company.

Joe had not been angry about it. "Neil is better at business," he had said.

The lawyer, Heather Howell, came into the library, and everyone sat down. Heather looked a little nervous.

"I'm afraid that we cannot read the will today," she said.

Judith looked at Caroline, who said nothing. Then, she looked at Maya and back at Heather. "Can you explain what's going on?" said Judith.

"We don't have the correct documents yet," said Heather. "Because Joe was murdered, we need to wait for the police to say that they've checked everything before we can open the envelope with the will."

"What do you mean, checked everything?" said Neil. "Do you mean to check that Joe is dead?"

Heather looked uncomfortable. "I'm sure that it's not a big problem. I'll contact you again when I have more information."

Everyone was silent as Heather left the room.

"I suppose that this is how lawyers are," Judith said. "I'm sure that they'll fix it soon."

Everyone got up to leave.

"Keep in contact, Maya," said Judith.

"I will," said Maya.

When Judith had left, Maya walked to her car and saw Caroline waiting beside it.

"Do you have a moment to talk?" asked Caroline.

"Not really," Maya thought. She wanted to leave immediately to start looking for Isabella and go to Leather and Lace. However, she agreed to take a walk with Caroline in the gardens, hoping that it would not take long.

"My father built that soccer field for Joe and Andrew. They loved soccer," Caroline said, as they walked toward it.

Maya nodded but did not say anything. She wanted Caroline to hurry up, but it was clear that Caroline wanted to tell her something important, so she had to be patient.

"Do you know much about my brother Andrew?" asked Caroline.

Although Maya said, "No," she actually knew the biggest secret about Andrew, because Joe had told her.

"The world thinks that my brother died because he fell off a boat at sea," Joe had said, *"but the truth is that Andrew jumped. It was **suicide**, Maya. But my family don't want anyone to know that."*

"Joe and Andrew loved each other," said Caroline. "They went to the same high school, Franklin Biddle Academy near Philadelphia. They lived together and played soccer on the same **team**." Then, Caroline turned to look directly at Maya. "Maya, what do you think about this . . . problem with the will?"

"I don't know," said Maya.

"Did you see Joe's body before the funeral?" asked Caroline.

Maya slowly shook her head. "No," she said.

"Neither did I," said Caroline, "although I did ask to see him. It was the same with Andrew. I didn't see his body, either."

This surprised Maya. "The police found Andrew's body, didn't they?"

"That's what I was told," Caroline said, "but I was young, and they never let me see him. Two of my brothers are dead, but I saw no bodies. It's like . . ." Caroline turned and stared straight into Maya's eyes. "It's like they could both be alive."

Maya did not move. "But they aren't alive, Caroline. And I was there when Joe died."

"But you didn't actually see him die, did you?" said Caroline. "You ran away before the third shot. And Isabella said that you had a fight with her. She said that you were screaming about seeing Joe on your nanny cam."

"Listen to me, Caroline. The police have been doing an **investigation**. They even found the two guys who were there in the park. Joe is dead."

Caroline was silent for a moment. Then, she said, "There's one more thing. Do you know the detective who's investigating Joe's death, Roger Kierce?"

"Yes," said Maya. "What about him?"

"This is going to sound crazy, but I found out that our family's private bank has been paying Kierce. He was paid nine thousand dollars a few times."

Maya stared at her. "Was this before or after Joe's death?"

"I'm positive that the first time was before," said Caroline.

"What's going on?" Maya thought. Caroline might be lying to her. She could ask Judith and Neil, but they could just lie, too. Until she could get more information, it was better to say nothing and carry on with her plan of talking to Isabella and going to Leather and Lace.

Maya went to Isabella's house and knocked on the door again. This time Hector opened it.

"Isabella isn't here. She's gone abroad," he said.

"That's a lie," thought Maya. "When will she be back?" she asked.

"She'll call you. Please stop coming here."

Maya had been sure that Hector would lie to her. Isabella was definitely not abroad. As Maya left, she passed by Hector's truck and put a **GPS tracker** on it. This way she could check where he was going and find Isabella.

The strip club, Leather and Lace, opened at eleven o'clock in the morning. There was a tall **security guard** at the door.

"I need to speak to the boss," Maya said.

She was taken into an office, where a woman was sitting behind a desk.

She smiled at Maya. "I'm Lulu. How can I help you?"

"My sister used to make phone calls to here," said Maya. "Her name was Claire Walker. Does that name mean anything to you?"

"No. And to be honest, if it did mean anything, I wouldn't

tell you. We keep things secret for our customers, Miss . . .?"

"My name's Maya Stern. And my sister was murdered four months ago. She had a secret phone, and the only calls that she made or received were from this place."

"I'm very sorry to hear about your sister," said Lulu. "But I can't help you. We don't keep our security camera videos for longer than two weeks, so there won't be anything from four months ago."

"Fine," said Maya, unhappily.

Lulu was already moving toward the door. "I'm sorry."

Maya walked out of the exit into the bright sun. What should she do now? She could go to the police, but that would mean talking to Kierce. Maya did not know whether to believe Caroline's story about him, but she was not ready to trust him. The only person she still trusted was Shane, who she was meeting tonight at the **gun range**. Maybe she would talk to him, but he was starting to ask too many questions . . .

She started walking toward her car, then stopped.

Across the parking lot she saw the red car that had followed her before. The license plate was the same. She opened her purse and took out another GPS tracker, but as she started walking toward the car a voice behind her said, "That's the wrong way."

It was the security guard.

"That area is only for people who are employed here," he said. "Your car is parked on the other side."

The security guard walked with Maya to her car and

waited for her to get in. She needed another plan. There was a factory building just down the road with some parking outside. If she parked there, she could watch the red car and follow it if the driver came back. So she drove her car there and waited.

After some time, a man came out of a side door of the strip club. He had a big beard, but his face reminded her of someone. He got into the red car and drove out of the parking lot.

Maya followed him, but after a few minutes she realized that her plan could not work. First, this man had followed her before, so he knew what her car looked like. Second, the security guard or Lulu had probably told the man about her visit. Third, maybe the driver had put a GPS tracker on her car earlier, so he would know that she was behind him.

Should she leave and come back another day with a new plan? No, Maya needed answers, so it was time to take action now. She increased her speed, drove around the car, and stopped in front of it. Taking her gun out of her purse, she got out of her car and into the passenger seat of the red one. As she closed the door she pointed the gun at the driver's head.

The man turned and smiled at her. "Hey, Maya. It's nice to finally meet you."

Maya stared at him in shock. It was Corey Rudzinski.

CHAPTER SIX
Corey the whistleblower

"Why have you been following me?" asked Maya.

"Put the gun down, Maya. Then, we can talk."

She moved her gun away from his head. "Did you know my sister?" she asked. Corey's smile disappeared, and, when she saw the **sadness** in his eyes, she realized that he *had* known Claire.

"Let's go back to Leather and Lace. Someone might notice us here," said Corey.

At the strip club, a security guard checked their faces on a camera before the door opened. They walked to a small private room at the back.

"Have a seat," said Corey. "I need to explain what I do."

"I understand what you do," said Maya. "You're a whistleblower. You think that secrets are bad, so you release them to the world, without troubling yourself about how the scandal could affect people."

"That's not far from the truth, actually," he said. "But people think that I want to destroy governments and companies. The truth is that I want to make them stronger by making them be honest and do the right thing. Businesses and governments lie; they pay people to hide their crimes. But imagine a world where that didn't happen. So I release their secrets, and with you it was the government killing civilians in a war . . ."

"That's not what we were doing," interrupted Maya.

"I know, I know, it was an accident," said Corey. "But I believe that people ought to know about these things."

"So how do you know my sister?"

"She contacted me," said Corey. "Several months before her death she sent me an email. She wanted to discuss you, Maya."

"Me? Are you saying that she sent you the video from my combat helicopter?" asked Maya.

"No," said Corey. "She contacted me *after* I released the video, because she was scared that I'd release the audio, too."

Maya was silent.

"You told Claire about it, didn't you, Maya?" he asked.

"Yes," Maya said. "I thought that we told each other everything, although now I'm not sure."

"She was trying to **protect** you by asking me not to release the audio," he said. "She argued with me about it, saying that you were only human, and it wasn't fair to punish you alone. She said that the real fault was with the government."

Maya nodded. "And if you released the audio, people would blame me instead of the government."

"Yes," said Corey. "However, there was something else. Claire worked for a big company that had its own secrets: the Burkett company."

Maya was starting to understand. "So you agreed not to release the audio, if she gave you information about the

COREY THE WHISTLEBLOWER

company. What were you investigating?"

"One of the Burkett family businesses is a medicine company called EAC," said Corey. "They're making a medicine to sell in Asia which isn't safe. People have died after taking it. The Burkett family argue that they tested the medicine, and they're blaming workers in Asia for making mistakes. But this is all lies. They must be paying people in those countries' governments to keep it a secret."

"Except you couldn't prove it, so you needed someone in the company, like Claire, to give you information. And that's what got her murdered," said Maya.

"She wanted to do it, Maya," said Corey, "and it wasn't just Claire. She was working with Joe, remember."

Corey seemed to think that this was the connection between Claire and Joe's deaths. "So you believe that the Burkett family killed Claire, and then Joe, to hide this secret?" said Maya. "I could agree with you about Claire, but not about Joe. He wouldn't want to destroy his family business, and the Burkett family would never kill one of their own kids."

"You may be right," Corey said. "But I think Claire discovered something else, too. Lulu told me that you found her secret phone. She used that to contact me, and several days before her death she called because she had something to show me."

Corey gave Maya a piece of paper with a name on it: Tom Douglass.

"Does this name mean anything to you?" he asked.

"I've never heard of him," said Maya. "Who is he?"

"He's a private detective," said Corey. "Claire found out that the Burketts were paying him nine thousand dollars every month. This seemed like too much money for an ordinary job, so Claire thought that something else was going on."

"Nine thousand dollars?" Maya thought. According to Caroline, the Burketts were paying Kierce the same amount.

"So why were the Burketts paying Tom Douglass?" Maya asked Corey.

"I don't know," he said. "We tried to talk to him, but he told us nothing. Maybe you could try?" He gave her Tom Douglass's work and home addresses, which were both in a small town called Livingston.

Maya left the strip club and drove to the office where Tom Douglass worked as a private detective. When she knocked on the door, a man walking past told her that Tom had not been there for weeks, so she decided to try his home, a five-minute drive away.

The Douglass house was blue, and there was a fishing boat beside the garage. A woman of about fifty opened the front door. "May I help you?" she asked.

Maya smiled and replied, "My name's Maya Stern. I'm looking for Tom Douglass."

The woman did not smile back. "He's not here. He might not be back for a while. I've seen you on the news. What do you want with my husband?"

"Can I come in?"

Inside the house, there were pictures of fishing boats on the walls. Mrs. Douglass led Maya into the living room and stood looking at her. Maya explained about the money being paid to her husband by the Burketts and asked what work he was doing for the family.

"I don't know," Mrs. Douglass replied.

"Something about that money worried my sister, Mrs. Douglass. And then, a few days after she had discovered it, she was murdered."

Mrs. Douglass's mouth opened in shock. "Do you think that my husband was involved? Tom's a good man."

"I didn't say that. But he was doing something for the Burkett family that was worth nine thousand dollars a month," said Maya. "Where is he, Mrs. Douglass? I need to speak to him."

It was clear that Mrs. Douglass did not want to answer Maya's question. "He's away," she said, and she opened the front door for Maya to leave. "I'll tell him that you visited."

Later that day, Maya went to the gun range to meet Shane.

"Are you ready to tell me what's going on?" Shane asked.

Maya was not ready. She wanted to protect Shane. She also worried that Corey would get scared and disappear again if he thought that other people knew about him. Instead she told Shane about Caroline.

"She told me that the family has been giving Kierce

money," said Maya. "And she said that they started paying him before Joe died."

This confused Shane. "Caroline must be wrong. Perhaps she's imagining things," said Shane. "Didn't you tell me once that she was a little mad? And now her brother has been murdered, which could make her more paranoid."

"I suppose that's possible," said Maya. "And she told me something else. You know that her brother Andrew died in high school."

"Yes. He fell off a boat into the sea," said Shane.

"Well, actually, he didn't fall. Joe told me that he jumped. He killed himself," said Maya.

"Oh wow," said Shane.

"And Caroline told me today that she wasn't allowed to see either Andrew's or Joe's bodies, so she's finding it hard to believe that they really died. And now she thinks that the family is paying the detective investigating Joe's death . . ." Maya stopped suddenly as a thought came to her. "Oh no . . ."

"What?" said Shane.

She was remembering the pictures and the fishing boat at Tom Douglass's house. Did Tom's work involve the sea?

"Shane," she said. "I need you to find out if the **Coast Guard** officer who investigated Andrew's death was a man called Tom Douglass."

CHAPTER SEVEN
Looking for Tom Douglass

The night was bad.

The sounds began their attack on her in the moments between being awake and asleep, becoming louder and louder. Maya pressed her hands against her head to make them stop, but she could not escape them.

She was woken by loud screams. As she opened her eyes, she realized that the screams were coming from her.

Someone was knocking on the front door. Then, Maya heard it open and a voice called, "Maya? Maya?"

As she was getting out of bed, the bedroom door opened. It was Shane. Maya had given him a key to the house for emergencies. He was holding Lily, who had **tears** on her face.

"She was at the top of the stairs," said Shane.

Maya went to take her daughter, but Lily pulled back from her.

"I'm sorry, Lily. Mommy had a bad dream," said Maya. She felt so guilty. "What kind of mother am I?" she thought.

They went downstairs to have breakfast. While they were eating, Shane looked at Maya. He knew what had happened.

"How bad was it?" he asked her.

"I'm fine," said Maya.

"You need to talk to someone, Maya, and get help."

Shane looked at Lily. "It's not just about you, now. You have a daughter."

"I'll fix things, Shane. Don't worry."

"Well, I'm here because I found out that you were correct about Tom Douglass," he said. "He *was* the Coast Guard officer who investigated Andrew Burkett's death. His report said that the death was an accident which probably involved **alcohol**. There was nothing about suicide. What's going on, Maya?"

"I don't know, but I'm going to find out," she said.

Maya took out her mobile phone and called the Douglass house. There was no answer, so she left a message before hanging up: "I know why the Burketts were paying your husband. Call me."

Shane looked at her. "Who told you about Tom Douglass?" he asked.

"It isn't important," said Maya. She had decided that she ought not to tell him about Corey.

"Really?" Shane did not look happy. He got up and started walking up and down the room. Then, he said, "I called Detective Kierce this morning. I wanted to know what kind of guy he was. He didn't tell me anything about the murder investigation, which makes me believe that he's honest, but he told me about the video with Joe. Why didn't you tell me about it?"

"I wanted to, but you already think that I'm crazy."

"No, I just want to help you," said Shane. "Tell me what happened."

So Maya explained everything about the nanny cam, the pepper spray, Joe's green shirt, and trying to find Isabella.

"It can't be an old video, because there's never been a camera on that bookshelf before," she said.

"OK, so the next possible idea is that Joe's still alive." Shane held up a hand to stop Maya saying anything. "I know that sounds mad, but let's just imagine. Perhaps Joe paid those two guys in the park to fire fake shots, and then paid Kierce to lie about it."

Maya shook her head. "Joe is dead, Shane."

"Or he's alive and playing some kind of **trick** on you."

Maya thought about this. "Or someone else is."

After Shane left, Maya received a call from Mrs. Douglass, who asked her to come back as soon as possible. But first Maya drove to Eddie's with Lily and explained to him about Tom Douglass.

"Can you look through Claire's stuff again to see if there's anything about Tom? Look at everything, like her tickets, documents, notebooks . . ." Maya said.

Eddie nodded. "I will."

Then, leaving Lily with Eddie, she drove straight to the Douglass house.

Mrs. Douglass had a nervous, worried look on her face when she opened the door.

"Is your husband home?" asked Maya.

"No," said Mrs. Douglass. "I got your phone message. What was Tom doing? Please tell me." A tear fell down her cheek. Maya felt sure that she was not lying, so she decided to be honest, too.

"Your husband was in the Coast Guard. He investigated the death of a young man called Andrew Burkett."

"Yes, I know," Mrs. Douglass replied. "That's how Tom met the Burkett family. They liked his work, so they gave him more jobs."

"I don't think so," said Maya. "I think that the family paid Tom to say that the death was an accident. I need to speak to your husband to find out why. So where is he?"

"I don't know. That's why I called you back. Tom's been **missing** for three weeks."

When she left the Douglass house, Maya saw on her phone that she had had a call from Leather and Lace, so she drove straight to the strip club. The security guard let her in and took her to the same private room at the back. Corey was inside.

"Did you visit Tom Douglass?" he asked.

"I went to his house, but he's been missing for three weeks," said Maya.

Corey looked at her. "Did you find out why the Burketts were paying him?"

"Not completely." Maya told him what she knew about the investigation into Andrew Burkett's death.

"OK, let's try and understand it all," said Corey. "Your sister starts investigating and finds out about the family paying Tom, and she gets killed. Then, your husband is killed, and Tom goes missing."

"But there's something else to think about," said Maya. "You don't murder someone to hide your son's suicide.

You might pay them to be silent, but you don't kill them."

Corey nodded. "And you don't kill your own son."

"We need to find Tom Douglass," said Maya. "Can you investigate his phone calls, emails, and bank account? We could find out where he might go."

"Yes," Corey said. "I can do that."

Maya looked at Corey for a few seconds. Then, she took a deep breath and asked him, "Corey, I know that you didn't release the audio from the helicopter video because of my sister, but was that the only reason? You missed the chance to get a lot of attention for your website with that audio."

"Do you think that I only care about attention?" he asked.

Maya just looked at him.

"I didn't release it because I'm a human with feelings, and because I knew that you'd feel so guilty already. Why should I punish you more?" Corey continued.

She made no reply.

"How do you live with what you did, Maya?"

If Corey wished for an answer to that question, he would have to wait a long time, along with everyone else.

"Contact me when you've found more information about Tom Douglass," she said.

CHAPTER EIGHT
Two more deaths

Maya went to Eddie's to pick up Lily. When she arrived, Alexa, Eddie, and Lily were running around the front garden. Maya listened to Lily's happy laugh and thought how different it sounded to the horrible noises that she heard almost every night. She made herself smile, parked the car, and got out.

Eddie walked over and put his hand on Maya's arm. "Do you have a second? I want to tell you something." He turned to his daughter. "Alexa, could you watch Lily for a few more minutes?"

"Sure, Dad," said Alexa.

Maya went inside with Eddie.

"I searched through Claire's stuff, and it looks like she visited Tom Douglass twice in one week. And after the second visit she didn't come straight home. First, she traveled south toward Philadelphia. I found a gas station receipt."

"Do you know any reason why she would go there?" asked Maya.

"No," said Eddie. "Does this remind you of anything?"

Maya shook her head and said, "No," but this was a lie. It did remind Maya of somewhere that Caroline had talked about. The high school where Andrew and Joe had gone, Franklin Biddle Academy, was near Philadelphia.

On the drive home, Maya received a call from Eileen.

"Can I come to yours?" Eileen asked. "I'll bring something for dinner."

"Of course," said Maya. "Is something wrong?"

"I'll be there in twenty minutes."

When Maya got home, Eileen was already waiting. Lily had fallen asleep in the back of the car.

"Let her sleep for a second," Eileen said. "We need to talk. And we have to stay outside, because it might not be safe to talk inside." She had tears on her face.

"What's wrong?" asked Maya.

"It's Robby," said Eileen. "He's been watching me. I made a big mistake when I bought the nanny cam. I got these by email, from an unknown address." Eileen reached into her purse, took out some photographs. The photos were of Eileen's living room and showed Eileen kissing a man on her couch. Maya's stomach dropped when she realized that the photos were from Eileen's nanny cam.

"So your ex-husband has the technology to watch and record you through the nanny cam?" asked Maya.

"Yes, it had to be him. Why didn't I check the nanny cams' **security**? I'm so sorry, Maya."

Maya thought about this new information. Could someone be watching her on her nanny cam, and had they put a fake video on it?

"What are you going to do about Robby?" asked Maya.

Eileen explained that she had given the photos to her lawyer and had called her internet company to check the security of her home internet.

That sounded like a good idea to Maya, so, half an hour after Eileen left, she called Shane.

"I need another favor," she said.

"That doesn't surprise me," replied Shane.

"Do you know anyone who can come and check whether someone is secretly recording me in my house?" she asked.

"I do," he replied. "I think you're being a little paranoid, but I'll come over with some guys tomorrow morning to check your house."

Maya thanked him and hung up. Then, she went online to find more information about Andrew Burkett. She found an old news story about his death, with the title: "Young Burkett son dies in the Atlantic Ocean."

According to the story, Andrew was last seen on the boat at 1 a.m. at the end of a party with family and friends, and he was reported missing to the police at 6 a.m. Joe had told Maya that some friends from their soccer team had been on the boat as well.

Next, Maya went to the Franklin Biddle Academy website and found a page with pictures of students at the school who had died. She found a photo of Andrew beside one of another student who had died in the same year. This student, called Theo Mora, had died on September 12th, which was only six weeks before Andrew died. Theo had been seventeen, like Andrew.

Maya searched for Andrew Burkett and Theo Mora's names together. She found the school sports website with team photographs and found Andrew and Theo in one of them. Two boys on the same soccer team had died less than two months from each other. Could that happen by chance? She looked at the rest of the photo and found Joe. This was no surprise as he had been team captain. She looked at his handsome, proud, and **confident** face. According to the news story about Andrew's death, there had been three other friends from the soccer team on the boat. Maya decided to write down the names of all the boys in the photo and try to find their phone numbers and emails. She could then contact them and find out who had been on the boat.

Maya thought about whether Claire had found the same information on the website or from Tom Douglass. She had probably driven to Franklin Biddle Academy to find out more. Is that what had gotten her killed?

The only way to know was to go down to Philadelphia. Maya had another difficult night and woke up the next day feeling extremely tired. As it was Sunday, both the Franklin Biddle Academy and Lily's day care center would be closed, so she decided to wait until Monday to drive to Philadelphia. A good soldier knows that it is important to rest when you have the chance, so she would wait a day and spend some time with her daughter.

Shane came at 8 a.m. with two guys who began to check her whole house for any technology that could secretly record or watch her. Shane picked up the nanny cam and saw that it was not **connected** to the internet.

"No one is watching you," he said. "Why won't you tell me everything that's going on, Maya?"

"I am telling you everything, Shane."

Shane looked unhappy. "Do you think that I'm stupid? Why did you ask me about Tom Douglass and Andrew Burkett? Is there some connection with Joe's murder?"

"I don't know yet," she said.

"So what are you going to do next?" he asked.

Tears almost came to her eyes, but she stopped herself from crying. "Nothing, Shane. It's Sunday and a beautiful fall day. I'm going to spend it with my daughter."

Shane's face changed. He smiled and his voice became soft. "You're right. We'll hurry up here and let you enjoy the rest of the day together."

The guys left, finding nothing in the house that could secretly record her. Then, Maya drove Lily to a farm, where they spent the day picking apples, feeding the animals, and eating ice cream. But Maya always felt more comfortable protecting people than enjoying herself with them, and she found it hard to relax.

CHAPTER NINE
Visiting Philadelphia

The next morning, Maya drove to Franklin Biddle Academy, which was an expensive private school. She entered the building, and a receptionist looked up at her.

"May I help you?" she asked.

"I'm Maya Burkett. I'd like to speak to the **headmaster**."

"Please have a seat."

She did not have to wait long before the headmaster arrived. He took both of her hands.

"My name is Neville Lockwood, Mrs. Burkett," he said. "And we're so sorry about your husband's death."

"Thank you, Mr. Lockwood."

He took her into his office, and they sat down at his desk.

"Joe was loved by everyone here," said the headmaster. "He was one of the best soccer players on his team and won many medals for this school."

"That's kind of you to say," she replied. "As you know, the Burkett family were proud to send their children to this school, although there has also been a lot of sadness here."

"Ah, yes. You're talking about your husband's brother, Andrew," he said. "It was such a terrible thing. Poor Judith, losing two sons."

"Yes," Maya said. "And what's strange is that now three boys from the same soccer team are dead. I'm talking now about Theo Mora. Do you remember him?"

The colour disappeared from Lockwood's face.

"How did Theo die?" asked Maya.

"Theo died of **alcohol poisoning**," the headmaster said. "He drank himself to death. Theo didn't usually drink much alcohol, but during one party he had too much. He fell into a basement, and he was found there, already dead, the next morning. Why are you asking about this now?"

"Didn't you ever think that it was strange that two young men who were in the same school and same soccer team died only months after each other?" she asked.

"Actually, I thought that there must definitely be a connection," Lockwood said.

This surprised Maya. "Can you explain?" she asked.

"They weren't just in the same school and soccer team; they also shared a room at school."

They were both silent. It was impossible that this was all just chance.

Lockwood explained to Maya that Andrew had been Theo's best friend. "Theo's death hurt him a lot, and he was extremely sad. Andrew wasn't like Joe. Joe was confident and wanted to win at everything, while Andrew was much more **sensitive**. We closed the school for a week after Theo died. When we opened it again, Andrew didn't come back. His mother felt that it would be best if he stayed at home for the rest of the semester. Some time later, the soccer team won a big competition between the schools in this area, and Joe and a few friends had a big party on the Burketts' boat."

"Do you know which boys?" asked Maya.

"I remember that one of them was Christopher Swain," he said. "Well, here's my idea: Andrew was a sensitive boy whose best friend died. He had to leave school and was finding life extremely difficult. Then, he went on the boat with his friends from the soccer team. Being there reminded him of his best friend. He drank a lot of alcohol, and he was in enormous pain . . ."

Lockwood stopped talking.

"Do you think that it was suicide?" asked Maya.

"Possibly," he said. "Or perhaps he drank too much and just fell over the edge of the boat."

"And then there's one more question: how do you explain the third death?" she asked. "I'm talking about Joe."

Lockwood stared at her. "What? Do you think that there's a connection between Andrew and Theo's deaths and your husband's murder, seventeen years later?"

"Yes, I do," she said.

There was nothing more to learn from the headmaster, so Maya left and sat in her car. She took out her phone and saw that Leather and Lace had called. Corey needed to speak to her. The strip club was two hours away, and she had other places to be. He would just have to wait. She searched online and found out that Theo's mother was called Raisa Mora and she lived in Philadelphia. Maya found her address and decided to visit her.

Raisa Mora's street was in a poor area of the city. Maya found the apartment and pressed the doorbell.

"Who is it?" said a woman's voice from the inside.

"My name is Maya, and I'd like to speak to you about your son Theo," said Maya.

The door suddenly opened. Raisa Mora had gray hair and looked tired. Maya could see that she worked as a waitress because she was still wearing her work clothes.

"Who are you?" she asked.

"My name is Maya Stern . . ." Then, Maya decided to correct herself and she added, "Maya Burkett."

This got the woman's attention.

"Your Joe's wife, aren't you? I saw on the news that the police have found the two men who murdered him."

"They didn't do it," said Maya. "I don't have time to explain, but I don't think that we know everything about your son's death."

"I don't understand," said Raisa. "Do you think there's a connection between Joe's murder and my Theo? What do you want to know?"

"Everything," said Maya.

"Come in then. I'm going to need to sit down."

The two women sat beside each other on an old couch. Raisa gave Maya a photograph showing a family of five people. A younger Raisa was standing next to a man with a mustache, with Theo and two smaller boys in front.

"That's Javier, Theo's father," said Raisa, pointing to the man. "He died two years after Theo died."

Then, Raisa told Maya her story.

"Javier came from Mexico, but we met in the USA and

VISITING PHILADELPHIA

moved to Philadelphia. He was a gardener, and he worked for some rich families. Javier used to talk to them about Theo." Raisa's face filled with sadness as she said her son's name. "Theo played sports, and he was smart and confident. We wished for him to have a successful career, but we couldn't afford an expensive private school. However, one of the families that Javier worked for managed to get Theo a place at Franklin Biddle Academy for free. Javier was so happy, but I was a little worried. He was a poor kid going to a rich kids' school."

Maya nodded with understanding.

Raisa continued. "One morning, Javier went to work. I was at home and the doorbell rang. It was the headmaster and another person with sad, serious looks on their faces. They told me that Theo had died from alcohol poisoning. They said that he wasn't found until the next morning, in a basement.

"But Javier didn't believe it," said Raisa. "Theo was the new kid in school. Javier thought that the other boys had made him drink too much alcohol. He wanted to go to the school and make them admit it, but I didn't think that would help. It wouldn't bring Theo back anyway."

"Mrs. Mora, do you remember Theo's best friend at Franklin Biddle, Andrew Burkett?" asked Maya.

"Yes, of course. He came to Theo's funeral with the other boys. Andrew was extremely sad, and then a few weeks later he fell off that boat. I didn't believe that it was an accident."

"I don't think that it was, either," said Maya.

"We went to Andrew's funeral," said Raisa. "Andrew had so much sadness about Theo. Maybe that's what killed him. However, Javier didn't believe that."

"What did he believe?" asked Maya.

"He said that people don't kill themselves because they feel sad. They do it because they feel guilty."

They were both silent. What had Andrew felt guilty about? Raisa looked at Maya.

"And now you're here. Do you know who killed my son?"

"I don't."

But Maya was starting to think that maybe she did.

CHAPTER TEN
Finding Tom Douglass

When Maya got back in her car, she just wanted to sit there and cry, but she did not have time. She called Eddie and asked him to pick Lily up from day care later and take her to his house. Then, she went online and searched for "Christopher Swain." She found an email address for him on the Franklin Biddle Academy website and sent him a short message.

My name is Maya Burkett. My husband was Joe. We must speak urgently. Please contact me as soon as you can.

She gave him her phone number and then drove to Leather and Lace.

Two hours later, Maya arrived at the strip club. She was getting out of her car when the passenger door opened, and Corey got in quickly.

"Drive to Livingston," he whispered.

Maya immediately started the car and drove out of the parking lot.

"That's where Tom Douglass lives, isn't it?" she said. "What's wrong?"

"I managed to get into Tom's email," Corey said. "He hasn't read or sent any emails for almost a month."

"That's when his wife said that he disappeared."

"Yes," said Corey. "Earlier today, Tom received an email about an unpaid bill for a **storage shed** that he rents in

Livingston. He might be hiding something in that storage shed, so we're going to investigate. I've brought ski masks and something to cut the lock."

When they arrived, Corey gave Maya a ski mask, but she shook her head. "People will notice us more if we wear them, and it's dark, anyway."

They found the storage shed in a parking lot behind an old car garage. The grass was long and there were old cars and broken car parts everywhere. Clearly, hardly anyone ever came here. As they got nearer the shed, there was an awful smell.

"Oh no," said Corey. "Let's leave."

"We need to see what it is. It might just be a dead animal," said Maya. "I'm going to open it."

She cut the lock. When the door opened, a human arm fell out.

"Oh God!" said Corey, holding his stomach.

Maya stepped toward the body. "Corey, you should leave if you're going to be sick. You don't want the police to know that you've been here. I'll manage this."

After Corey left, Maya waited twenty minutes before phoning the police. When they arrived, her story was that she had received a call from an unknown number. She said that the caller had told her that Tom's body was here. Maya realized that the police would talk to Mrs. Douglass, so she told them the truth about visiting her.

"My sister was murdered and she spoke to Tom not long before her death. I wanted to know why," Maya said.

The police took her to the station for more questions and Detective Kierce arrived. Maya remembered what Caroline had said about the family paying him.

He smiled. "You keep finding yourself around dead bodies, don't you, Maya? First there was Joe, and now it's this man."

Maya looked at him. "Do you think that I murdered this man? But clearly he was killed weeks ago, and why would I stay and call the police if I'd killed him?"

Kierce had no reply. Instead he asked about the caller.

"So someone told you about your sister and Tom, and then the same person told you about this storage shed. You're hiding something, Maya. I think that you've been lying to me since the beginning."

Maya had had enough of this conversation, so she decided to accuse Kierce. "Caroline Burkett tells me that her family has been paying you money."

Kierce smiled. "That's a lie. But I'm not sure if Caroline was lying to you or you're lying to me now."

The police had no reason to keep Maya, so they let her leave. She went to Eddie's house to pick up Lily. When she got home, she put Lily to bed and sat down on a chair near her, watching her. For a moment, she felt wonderfully peaceful and normal. She wanted to stay here, in this room with her daughter, forever.

If Maya slept, the sounds would just come back, so she picked up a pen and notebook and started writing some letters.

In the morning, she walked down to the basement of the house and went to her gun safe. She unlocked it with her fingerprint and took out one of her guns. Then, she took the others out and carefully cleaned each one. She was always careful like this with her guns, and it had probably saved her life . . . or destroyed it.

After she finished, she reached into the back of the safe and pressed her hand against something which clicked.

A secret compartment opened, where Maya always kept two extra hidden guns. As she looked at them, she was reminded of her grandmother's secret compartment where she found Claire's phone.

Maya jumped in surprise as her phone rang. She pressed the answer button and said, "Hello?"

"Is this Maya Burkett?" said a man's voice.

"Yes. Who is this?"

"My name is Christopher Swain. You sent me an email."

"Yes," said Maya. "I wanted to ask you some questions about Joe and his brother Andrew."

Christopher was silent for a moment. Then, he said, "Joe's dead, right?"

"Yes," she replied.

"OK, I'll talk to you, but not on the phone," he said.

He gave her an address and hung up. Maya put her gun in her belt, then took the nanny cam from the living room and put it in the back of her car. She did not want it in the house any more. Then, after taking Lily to day care, she drove to Christopher Swain's address.

CHAPTER ELEVEN
What happened to Andrew?

Maya drove along a road that went through a large wood before arriving at Christopher Swain's address. There was a group of buildings with a gate and security cameras.

A security guard came to take her inside one of the buildings.

"What is this place?" asked Maya.

"It's a **recovery center**," said the man. "People come here to get better from problems that they have, like with alcohol."

A woman met them at the door and took Maya into a large living room, where Christopher Swain was waiting. He stood up and nervously said hello.

They sat down beside each other, and Christopher looked out of the window. Then, he said, "Joe was so confident and full of life. I can't believe that he's dead."

"Christopher," Maya said. "You were on the boat the night that Andrew died."

He did not move.

"What really happened?" she asked.

A tear dropped down Christopher's cheek. "I didn't see it, Maya."

"But you know something?" she said. "Did Andrew really fall?"

"I think . . ." he whispered, before taking a deep breath

and starting again. "I think that Joe pushed him off the boat."

Maya looked at him silently. Christopher held the arms of his chair as he told Maya his story.

"It started when Theo Mora came to Franklin Biddle Academy. You might think that we, the rich kids, were horrible to Theo because his family was poor. But he was a funny, confident guy, and we all liked him. He was also a fantastic soccer player, which was possibly the problem."

"What do you mean?" asked Maya.

"Joe always wanted to be the best player on the team. I had known Joe since we were kids, and I saw what he could do when he was angry. Once, he attacked a kid so badly that the kid had to go to hospital. A year later, this girl that Joe liked planned to go to a dance with another boy. Two days before the dance, there was a fire in the boy's classroom and he hardly escaped alive."

"No one reported this to the police?" asked Maya.

"You didn't know Joe's dad," said Christopher. "He was a frightening man. He could scare anyone, and the family also paid people to stay quiet. Joe usually hid his anger, but sometimes I saw it appear . . ."

The tears started coming again.

"Do you know why I'm in this recovery center?" he said. "I'm here because of Joe. At first, I never used to drink more than a beer, but then I couldn't stop myself . . ."

"Christopher," Maya interrupted. "What happened to Theo?"

"We'd only planned for it to be a funny trick. That's what Joe said anyway, and at first Theo believed it, too. Joe was the leader; Andrew and I were always the followers. Four of us held Theo in a chair while Joe got a bottle of beer and started **pouring** it into Theo's mouth. We were all laughing and shouting, "Drink! Drink! Drink!" Theo's eyes began to look really scared. Then, Joe changed the beer to a much stronger alcohol, and I remember Andrew saying, 'Wait, Joe, stop …' Suddenly, Theo's leg started shaking, like something was seriously wrong with him . . ."

Christopher started to cry. Maya had to wait for him to stop.

"So you moved his body into the basement?" she asked after a while.

"Joe did that," Christopher said. "And he made Andrew help him. I think that was too much for Andrew."

Javier Mora had been right. Andrew had felt guilty.

"So what happened?" Maya asked.

"We had to keep the secret," said Christopher. "I tried to live an ordinary life, but nothing was the same. That's when I started drinking more alcohol."

"So what about the boat six weeks later?" asked Maya.

"It was the first time that we'd all been together since Theo's funeral," he said. "Andrew looked awful. He couldn't sleep or eat. He kept crying and saying that we had to go to the police. He went outside on the boat, and several minutes later Joe followed him. That's all I saw."

"And you never told anyone for all these years?" asked Maya.

Christopher nodded.

"So why are you able to tell the truth now?" she asked.

"Because Joe is dead," he said. "And I don't have to be scared of him any more. I finally feel safe."

Maya heard Christopher Swain's words in her head as she walked back to her car.

"Because Joe is dead . . ."

She immediately thought of seeing Joe in the nanny cam video. There were three ways to explain it. First, Joe could still be alive. Second, Maya's mind was **tricking** her, and she had imagined seeing him. Her PTSD and the shock of Claire's murder could make that happen. Finally, perhaps someone had recorded a fake video. She needed to find Isabella, and make her tell the truth.

Maya got into her car and looked on her phone to check the GPS tracker that she had put on Hector's truck. It was parked outside an address in Paterson, a town in New Jersey. Perhaps Isabella was hiding there.

Suddenly, her phone rang. It was Shane.

"What have you done, Maya?" he asked.

"What are you talking about?" she said.

"I spoke to Detective Kierce. He found out that I tested that bullet for you. He told me that the same gun killed Claire and Joe. How is that possible, Maya?"

"Shane, you just have to trust me, OK?" she said.

"You keep saying that, Maya," he replied. "Tell me what's going on!"

"I have to go, Shane." She hung up and closed her eyes.

"Forget about it," she told herself, but the call from Shane had shaken her.

Then, she called Eddie, asking him to meet her outside Lily's day care center.

When Eddie's car arrived at the day care center, she got into the passenger seat.

"What's happening, Maya?" he asked.

"I need you to pick Lily up and look after her again."

Eddie looked at her. "Do you know who killed Claire and Joe?"

"Yes," she said.

"But you won't tell me?" he said.

"Not yet, no. I don't have time, and Claire would want me to protect you."

"Maybe I don't want to be protected," he argued. "I can help you."

"You can help me by picking up Lily," she said.

As he turned to open the car door, she put an envelope into his bag without him seeing. Then, she got out, too.

"I love you, Eddie."

"I love you, too, Maya."

She watched him go inside the day care center, then got into her car and drove away.

CHAPTER TWELVE
Finding Isabella

Maya found Hector's truck parked outside a tall building. She decided to wait for him, and make him tell her where Isabella was.

After half an hour, Hector and Isabella appeared at the door of the building. Maya took out her gun as she watched them get into his truck. Now was her chance.

She hurried to the truck, got in behind them and pushed the gun into the back of Hector's neck.

"Put your hands up where I can see them."

They both slowly lifted their hands. Maya reached for Isabella's purse and looked inside. There was a mobile phone and the pepper spray. Then, she noticed something green on the floor by her feet. It was Joe's shirt.

"Explain," ordered Maya.

Neither of them spoke. So Maya started talking instead.

"Hector is as tall as Joe. So I suppose he put on Joe's shirt. You found an old video of Joe and put his face on Hector's body in that nanny cam video. Am I right?"

"We have nothing to say to you," said Isabella.

Maya hit the gun hard on Hector's nose. Blood started pouring out of it.

"Maybe I won't kill him," she said to Isabella, "but the first bullet goes into his shoulder, and the next into his knee. So start talking."

FINDING ISABELLA

"OK!" said Isabella. "We did it because you killed Joe!"

"Who told you that?" asked Maya.

"Our mother. She said that you killed Joe, and we had to help prove it by making the fake video for your nanny cam. I had to make you believe that you were the only person who saw Joe on it."

"You wanted me to feel crazy, so that I'd make a mistake?" said Maya. "Wait, how did you know that I had a nanny cam?"

Isabella laughed. "Suddenly, the day after the funeral there's a new digital picture frame with photos of your family. You're the only mother that I know who doesn't have pictures of your daughter in the house. I'm not stupid. Of course it had to be a nanny cam."

Maya remembered that Isabella was always smiling in the nanny cam videos.

"And was it your mother's idea to use the pepper spray?"

"I needed to get the SD card," said Isabella, "so that you couldn't show it to people. You had to be the only one to see 'Joe.'"

Maya nodded. "You wanted me to stop trusting myself."

But Maya stopped talking because Shane was standing in front of the truck.

"If you move," Maya said to Hector and Isabella, "I'll shoot you dead."

She got out of the car and walked toward Shane.

"What are you doing?" he asked.

"They tricked me, Shane. Hector wore Joe's clothes, and

they made a fake video for the nanny cam."

"So Joe really is dead. He was never tricking you," said Shane.

"How did you find me, Shane?"

"I put a GPS tracker on your car," he said.

"Why did you do that?"

"Because you've been acting crazy, Maya. You have to see that."

Maya looked back at the truck. Hector and Isabella were still inside. Then, she looked back at Shane.

"I need to tell you something," she said.

"About the bullets?"

"No, about the helicopter video in Iraq."

Shane looked confused. "What about it?"

"We'd already lost some good men. I didn't want to lose any more. We could hear those two young soldiers screaming through their radios. They needed us to save them. But we were waiting for our guys on the radio to tell us that we could shoot the black car."

"Yes," said Shane. "We had to check that the people in the car weren't civilians, or even kids. We weren't sure whether they were enemies, but it was hard to hear the radio clearly. It wasn't our fault that civilians died."

"Except I did hear it, Shane," Maya said. "The radio guys told us to wait, but I didn't. I couldn't let our two boys die down there, so I shot a missile at the car and destroyed it, despite the radio message."

"What . . . what are you talking about?" Shane was

shaking his head. "But I heard..."

"No, you didn't hear anything, Shane," she said. "I told you that they'd allowed us to shoot. You didn't hear it yourself. Remember?"

Shane stared at her. "Why did you do it?" he said.

"Because I didn't care about the civilians. I cared about our boys."

"Oh God, Maya."

"That's what I chose to do, Shane. I wanted to save our boys, even if those civilians had to die. I just didn't care any more. Do you think that I have those horrible dreams every night because I feel guilty? No, I have them because I *don't* feel guilty. Because I know that I'd do it again. Every night, I hear the sounds from that helicopter."

"And every night you kill those civilians again," he said. "Oh, Maya." He stepped toward her to hug her, but she stepped back.

"There's something else," she said. "Kierce told you that Joe and Claire were killed by the same gun."

"Yes, which you never told me," he said. "But Maya, you gave me the bullet to test *before* Joe was shot. You told me to check whether it was from the same gun that killed Claire. And it was. So how did you have the bullet *before* Joe was murdered?"

"There's only one possible way," Maya said.

Shane shook his head, but he already knew.

"I killed him," Maya said. "I killed Joe."

CHAPTER THIRTEEN
The truth about the Burketts

Maya drove Hector's car to the Burketts' house. Shane was holding Isabella and Hector to stop them telling the Burketts that she was coming. Before reaching the house, Maya called Lulu from Leather and Lace one more time and asked for her help with something.

After she hung up, she parked the car by the side of the house and went inside through the unlocked kitchen door, without making a sound. She entered the living room, moving first to a bookshelf, before sitting down in the dark to wait.

She started remembering the past, how she and Joe had not known each other for long before they got married. She remembered coming home from Iraq after Claire's death and how Joe was then. He had talked a lot about how he hated guns and did not like her keeping them in the house. But despite hating guns, he had always wanted to be able to open the safe with his own fingerprint, saying that there might be an emergency. At that time, she kept two Smith and Wesson 686 revolvers in the safe, one of them in the secret compartment. One day, when she opened the secret compartment, she immediately knew that someone had used the hidden Smith and Wesson 686. It had not been carefully cleaned.

Only one other person could open that safe. Maya did

not want to admit it to herself, but she guessed the truth. So she gave Shane a bullet from that gun to test, and found out that it was the gun that had killed Claire.

Joe had killed Claire.

Was there a chance that she was wrong? She had to prove it, so she moved the two Smith and Wesson 686 revolvers, putting the one that Joe had *not* used in the secret compartment. She took all the bullets out of the other guns, so that Joe would definitely take that one. Then, she called him.

"I know what you did," she said.

"What are you talking about?" he asked.

"I can prove it," she said. "Meet me in Central Park."

She arrived in the park first and saw two guys that she could blame for the murder. If she told the police that they were wearing ski masks, they would not be sent to prison. The police would never be able to prove that these guys were the murderers.

Then, Joe arrived in the park.

"I know that you killed my sister, and I want you punished for it," she said. He pulled out the Smith and Wesson 686 that he had taken from the hidden compartment. He was smiling as he pointed it at her chest, but his smile changed to shock when the gun did not work.

"I've taken out the **firing pin**," said Maya.

"It doesn't matter. You'll never prove that I killed Claire," he said.

"I know," she said. Then, she lifted her gun, which was

the Smith and Wesson 686 that had killed Claire. She shot him three times in the shoulder, neck, and chest, making it look like a killer with less experience of guns than her.

As he was dying, Maya hugged Joe to get plenty of his blood on her shirt, then put both guns in her purse and ran out of the park screaming for help. Later, she threw the revolver that she had used to shoot Joe into the river. She put the firing pin back in the other one and put it in the safe. This was the one that Kierce took for testing, which had no connection with either murder.

Maya knew that if the same gun had killed both Claire and Joe, no one would think that she had killed Joe. She had been abroad when Claire was murdered, so the police would think that she had not killed Joe, either.

And then that nanny cam video changed everything.

From inside the Burketts' living room, Maya heard a car arrive. She stayed in her chair as the door opened and Judith came in with Neil and Caroline. Judith switched on the lights and screamed.

"My God!" she said. "You scared me to death, Maya. What are you doing here?"

"Joe isn't alive," said Maya. "You just wanted me to believe that to make me paranoid and see how I would react. First you told Isabella, her mother, and her brother to put that video on the nanny cam. Then, you told Caroline to talk to me about believing that her brothers were alive and that Detective Kierce was being paid. That was all lies, wasn't it?"

FOOL ME ONCE

Judith looked at her children and then back at Maya. "There's nothing wrong with that," she said. "There's no law against trying to catch a killer."

"How did you know that I killed Joe?" asked Maya.

"I just knew. A mother knows," said Judith.

"No, Judith. You knew that I had a reason to do it."

Caroline said, "What's she talking about, Mom?"

"Joe murdered my sister," said Maya.

"That's not true," said Caroline.

"Yes, it is," said Maya. "And your mother knew about it."

Caroline looked at her mother, who was still looking at Maya.

"Claire was trying to destroy the family business," said Judith. "Joe just tried to stop her. He went too far, I admit, but she was the enemy. You were a soldier, Maya. So you understand that you have to attack the enemy."

Maya felt her anger grow. "You stupid, awful woman."

"Hey!" It was Neil speaking. "Don't talk to my mother like that."

"You just admitted that you killed Joe, Maya," said Judith. "You'll go to prison."

"You don't understand," said Maya. "He didn't just kill my sister. He killed Theo Mora."

"That was an accident," said Judith.

"He killed Tom Douglass," said Maya.

"You can't prove that," said Judith.

"And he killed his own brother."

Everyone stopped. For a few seconds, they were all silent.

Caroline turned to Judith. "Mom, that's not true, is it?"

"Of course it's not true," said Judith, but her voice was shaking a little.

"I visited Christopher Swain today, Judith," said Maya. "He told me what happened on the boat. Andrew told the others that he wanted to go to the police about Theo's death. He went outside, and Joe followed him."

Caroline started crying. Neil looked scared.

"That doesn't mean that Joe killed him," said Judith. "That's just your mad idea."

"Joe told me that it was suicide," said Maya, and Judith nodded. "Except that's not what happened. Joe and Andrew went out at one o'clock, but nobody reported Andrew missing until six o'clock. If Joe saw Andrew jump, why wouldn't he report it immediately?"

Judith's eyes opened wide, and she dropped to her knees. It was clear that she had never admitted to herself before that Joe had done it. Then, she started to cry like a dying animal. "It can't be true."

"It's true," said Maya. "Joe killed Theo Mora, Andrew, Claire, and Tom Douglass. How many more did he kill? How many kids in school did he attack? His father saw it, which is why he gave control of the company to Neil. Everyone will find out now. You were the mother of a murderer, Judith."

"And you'll go to prison for life for his murder," said Judith.

"Probably," said Maya. "But everything will also be released about the Burkett medicine company EAC, so it's the end for you, too."

"There must be some way to escape all this," said Judith. "We can make a plan, Maya. Let's blame the EAC company scandal on Joe, and we won't tell the police about you killing him."

"It's too late for that, Judith," said Maya.

"She's right, Mom."

It was Neil, who was standing behind Maya, pointing a gun in her direction. "I have a better idea," he said to Maya. "You stole Hector's car and came into our house, probably with a gun. I could kill you now, and we'd say that we were protecting ourselves."

Neil looked at his mother, who smiled, and Caroline nodded. The whole family had agreed.

Neil shot Maya three times.

"The same number of times that I shot Joe," she thought.

Maya fell to the ground and heard voices.

"No one will ever know . . ."

"Check her pockets. Where's her gun?"

Maya smiled and looked toward the bookshelf.

"What's she smiling about . . . ?"

"What's that on the bookshelf? It looks like . . ."

"Oh no . . ."

Maya's eyes closed. She waited for the sounds of helicopters, guns, and screaming, but they did not come. They never came again.

It was dark and then silent. Finally, there was peace.

CHAPTER FOURTEEN
Twenty-five years later

The elevator doors are closing when I hear a voice say my name.

"Shane?"

It's Eileen. I hold the doors open for her.

"It's been a long time. You look good, Shane," she says, hugging me.

"So do you, Eileen."

People around the world saw the video from the Burketts' house all those years ago, from the nanny cam that Maya put on the bookshelf in their living room. So let me explain the rest. Maya had called Lulu at Leather and Lace, who worked with Corey Rudzinski. She got Lulu to record everything that happened in that living room through the nanny cam. The whole world was able to watch what happened, although no one was ready to see a murder right before their eyes.

When the elevator doors open again, Eileen and I get out and walk through the hospital.

We enter the room where Eddie, his new wife, Selina, and Alexa and Daniel are standing around the bed. We were never sure whether Maya knew that she would die that night, but she had left Eddie a letter. She told him to take care of Lily if anything happened to her.

TWENTY-FIVE YEARS LATER

Lily is lying in the bed, holding her new baby. Her husband is by her side.

"Hello, Shane," says Lily. "Would you like to hold her? We called her Maya."

I feel tears in my eyes as I nod.

Maya and I saw a lot of death. She believed that people die and are gone forever, with nothing left. But, looking at this baby, it feels like Maya is still here.

During-reading questions

CHAPTER ONE

1. Why does Maya say, "It's my fault" at the funeral, do you think?
2. Why does Eileen think that Maya needs a nanny cam?

CHAPTER TWO

1. Why is it possible for Shane to get information for Maya? Why is he unhappy about doing this, do you think?
2. Why does Maya hear the sounds from the video when she tries to sleep?

CHAPTER THREE

1. How is Kierce sure that Maya did not kill Claire or Joe?
2. What is Maya thinking about Isabella when she says, "Wow"?

CHAPTER FOUR

1. Why does Maya need to find out if she can trust Eileen?
2. Why is Eddie's house still full of boxes of Claire's stuff, do you think?

CHAPTER FIVE

1. What kind of help does Maya need, according to Judith?
2. Why does Caroline say that Joe and Andrew could be alive?

CHAPTER SIX

1. Why did Corey and Claire start working together?
2. Why doesn't Maya want to tell Shane about Corey?

CHAPTER SEVEN

1. What does Corey want to know when he asks Maya, "How do you live with what you did?"

CHAPTER EIGHT

1. How does Shane know that no one is watching Maya through the nanny cam?
2. Why does Maya almost start crying at the end of the chapter, do you think?

CHAPTER NINE

1. Why does the headmaster think that Andrew killed himself?
2. Why didn't Javier believe that Andrew killed himself because he was sad?

CHAPTER TEN

1. How do Kierce and Maya feel about each other now?
2. Why didn't the police keep Maya in the police station?

CHAPTER ELEVEN

1. Why didn't Joe like Theo being good at soccer?
2. Why does Maya feel shaken by Shane's call, do you think?

CHAPTER TWELVE

1 Who was the fake Joe in the video?
2 What is different about Maya's story about the helicopter video now?

CHAPTER THIRTEEN

1 How did Maya know that Joe had taken her gun and killed Claire?
2 Why does Judith drop to her knees and start crying?

CHAPTER FOURTEEN

1 Why does Shane feel like Maya is still here, do you think?

After-reading questions

1 In Chapter Five, was there really a problem with the will, do you think?
2 In Chapter Thirteen, how did the Burketts try to make Maya admit to killing Joe?
3 Look back at your answer to Before-reading question 3. How was Maya's PTSD shown in the story?

Exercises

CHAPTER ONE

1 Match the words with their definitions in your notebook.
Example: 1 – b

1 nanny cam
2 bullet
3 prove
4 scandal
5 investigate
6 revolver

a something that a lot of people talk about because they think it is wrong
b a video camera that you can put in your house to record a person's activities while they are taking care of your child
c to try to find out information or the truth about something, for example, a crime
d a small metal ball that comes out of a gun
e a small gun
f to show that something is true

CHAPTER TWO

2 Write the correct verb form, *past simple* or *past perfect*, in your notebook.

1 Before Corey Rudzinski released the video, Maya and Shane **flew / had flown** army combat helicopters.
2 While Maya was in the car after Alexa's soccer game, she **noticed / had noticed** the red car behind her.
3 A couple of weeks before Shane came to talk to Maya, she **gave / had given** him a bullet to do a test on.
4 Maya went online and **watched / had watched** the video again.

CHAPTER THREE

3 Are these sentences *true* or *false*? Write the correct answers in your notebook.

1 Isabella attacks Maya. *true*
2 Maya shows Kierce the nanny cam video.
3 The police have found the gun that killed Joe.
4 The police do not know who killed Claire.
5 Kierce thinks that Maya killed Joe.
6 Joe and Claire knew each other.

CHAPTERS FOUR AND FIVE

4 Which word is closest in meaning? Write the correct word in your notebook.

1 paranoid   **happy / *worried* / angry**
2 find out   **discover / talk / look**
3 hang up   **start talking / keep talking / stop talking**
4 compartment   **box / table / floor**
5 will   **document / book / website**
6 team   **person / group / place**

CHAPTERS SIX AND SEVEN

5 Complete these sentences in your notebook, using the names from the box.

| Corey | Maya | Shane | Claire | Mrs. Douglass |

1 ...*Corey*... believes that the world would be better if there were fewer secrets in big companies.
2 .... found out secrets about the Burkett family businesses.
3 .... does not want to talk to Maya at first.
4 .... is worried about Maya and wants to help her more.
5 .... does not seem to believe that Joe could be alive.

CHAPTERS EIGHT AND NINE

6 Complete these sentences with the correct word in your notebook.

| however | since | although | neither | whether |

1 Maya remembers that Joe's high school is in Philadelphia. ...*However*..., she doesn't tell Eddie this.
2 Maya wants Shane to check .... anyone could watch her through her nanny cam.
3 .... Maya will not tell him everything that she knows, Shane is unhappy with her.
4 .... the headmaster said that Theo had died from alcohol poisoning, Javier Mora did not believe that this was true.
5 .... Maya nor Raisa think that Andrew's death was an accident.

CHAPTERS TEN AND ELEVEN

7 Make these sentences reported speech in your notebook.

1 "Drive to Livingston," said Corey to Maya. *Corey told Maya to drive to Livingston.*
2 "You should leave if you're going to be sick," said Maya to Corey.
3 "I think that you've been lying to me since the beginning," said Kierce to Maya.
4 "I think that Joe pushed him off the boat," said Christopher to Maya.
5 "I saw what he could do when he was angry," said Christopher to Maya.
6 "You can help me by picking up Lily," said Maya to Eddie.

CHAPTERS TWELVE TO FOURTEEN

8 Put the sentences in the correct order in your notebook.

a The world learns the truth about Maya and the Burketts. ....
b The nanny cam video with the fake Joe is made. ....
c Maya looks in her safe and knows that her gun has been used. ...*1*.....
d Maya tells Shane the truth. ....
e Maya and Judith admit everything to each other. ....
f Maya meets Joe in Central Park. ....

Project work

1 Imagine that you are Shane. Write a diary entry about your friendship with Maya.
2 Write a review of the book. Did you like it? Why/Why not? Remember not to tell your readers what happens at the end of the book.
3 Imagine that you are a journalist who saw the nanny cam video from the Burketts' living room. Write a newspaper report about the story.
4 What did Maya say to Eddie in the letter that she left for him, do you think? Write her letter.

An answer key for all questions and exercises can be found at **www.penguinreaders.co.uk**

Glossary

alcohol (n.)
Alcohol is in drinks like beer and wine.

alcohol poisoning (n.)
a serious illness that someone gets if they drink too much *alcohol*

audio (n.)
sounds that someone has recorded

basement (n.)
part of a building that is underground

blame (v.)
to say that someone did something wrong

bullet (n.)
a small metal ball that comes out of a gun very fast

captain (n.)
a leader of soldiers and officers in an army

career (n.)
the most important job or jobs that you do through your life

civilian (n.)
a person who is not in the army

Coast Guard (n.)
military people who watch the sea for ships that are in danger and to make sure that the laws of the ocean are obeyed

combat helicopter (n.)
A *helicopter* is like a small plane. A *combat helicopter* is used in war.

compartment (n.)
part of a piece of furniture that you can put things in

confident (adj.)
You are *confident* when you know that you can do things well and you are not afraid or worried.

connect (v.) **connection** (n.)
to put things together. If things, ideas or people like each other, they may have a *connection*. If people know each other, or know the same people, there is a *connection* between them.

day care center (n.)
a place where people take care of young children during the day, because their parents are at work

destroy (v.)
to damage something so much that it is completely broken

digital picture frame (n.)
You put a picture in a *picture frame* on a wall. A *digital picture frame* shows lots of changing photos from your cell phone.

ex-husband (n.); **ex-soldier** (n.)
Ex- means in the past, but not anymore.

fake (adj.)
not real

fault (n.)
If a bad thing has happened because of something that you did, it is your *fault*.

find out (v.)
to discover a piece of information

fingerprint (n.)
the mark made by the end of your finger when you touch something. You can sometimes use a *fingerprint* to open a lock or to unlock your cell phone.

firing pin (n.)
in a gun, the part that makes the *bullet* shoot out

funeral (n.)
when people come together after someone's death

government (n.)
a group of people who decide what must happen in a country

GPS tracker (n.)
technology that helps people to find you anywhere in the world. *GPS* is short for Global Positioning System.

gun range (n.)
a place where people can practice shooting

hang up (v.)
to end a phone call

headmaster (n.)
a man whose job is to manage a school

hide (v.)
You *hide* something because you do not want people to find it or see it.

hug (v.)
to put your arms around a person because you love them or like them

investigate (v.); **investigation** (n.)
to try to *find out* information or the truth. This is an *investigation*.

involve (v.)
If an activity *involves* something, that thing is an important part of the activity.

license plate (n.)
the numbers and letters on the front and back of a car

military (adj.)
Military people or things are used in a war.

missile (n.)
something that is used in war to damage a place or building

missing (adj.)
If a person or thing is *missing*, you cannot find them.

nanny (n.)
a person whose job is to look after another person's children

nanny cam (n.)
a video camera that you can put in your house while the *nanny* is taking care of your child

paranoid (adj.)
Someone who is *paranoid* believes that other people or things want to harm them.

pepper spray (n.)
Someone shoots *pepper spray* into the face of another person, often to *protect* themselves. It makes your eyes, skin and throat burn.

pour (v.)
to put water, beer, milk, etc. into something

protect (v.)
to take care of something or someone and stop bad things from happening to them

prove (v.)
to show that something is true

PTSD (n.)
an illness in your mind after a very frightening experience. *PTSD* is short for Post-Traumatic Stress Disorder.

recovery center (n.)
a place where people go to get better from problems, for example, drinking too much *alcohol*

release (v.)
to make it possible for people to watch a video or listen to some *audio*

remind (v.)
to make you remember something

revolver (n.)
a small gun

sadness (n.)
feeling sad

safe (n.)
a strong metal box with a special lock. You keep money in it.

scandal (n.)
something that a lot of people talk about because they think it is wrong

SD card (n.)
a small piece of plastic that can hold computer information

security (n.)
things that people have done to *protect* you and keep you safe

security camera (n.)
a video camera that records people's activities.

security guard (n.)
a person whose job is to *protect* a place and the people who go there

sensitive (adj.)
A *sensitive* person feels things more strongly than other people. They sometimes feel shy or worried.

shot (n.)
the sound you hear when someone shoots a gun

ski mask (n.)
a type of hat. It covers most of the head, neck, and face.

state (n.)
part of a large country. There are fifty *states* in the USA.

storage shed (n.)
a small building where you store (= keep) things

strip club (n.)
A *club* is a place where people dance and drink at night. In a *strip club*, a person (usually a woman) dances without their clothes.

suicide (n.)
If a person dies by *suicide*, they kill themselves.

team (n.)
a group of people who play sport or work together

tear (n.)
a small amount of water that comes out of your eyes when you cry

trick (n. and v.)
If someone *tricks* you or plays a *trick* on you, they make you believe something that is not true.

whistleblower (n.)
a person who tells the public about something that is happening that is wrong or against the law

will (n.)
a document that gives information about who will get your money after you die